D0116209

This book belongs to

_____

VOLUME
14

DONALD
CRIES "WOLF!"

WALT DISNEY FUN-TO-READ LIBRARY

®

A BANTAM BOOK
TORONTO ● NEW YORK ● LONDON ● SYDNEY ● AUCKLAND

Donald Cries "Wolf!" A Bantam Book/January 1986 All rights reserved. Copyright © 1986 The Walt Disney
Company.   This book may not be reproduced, in whole or in part, by mimeograph or any other means.

ISBN 0-553-05591-7

Published simultaneously in the United States and Canada. Bantam Books are published by Bantam Books, Inc. Its
trademark, consisting of the words "Bantam Books" and the portrayal of a rooster, is Registered in U.S. Patent and
Trademark Office and in other countries. Marca Registrada. Bantam Books, Inc., 666 Fifth Avenue, New York,
New York 10103. Printed in the United States of America 0 9 8 7 6

One day, Mickey and Donald started
out for the woods. They were going camping.

"Donald, this is the perfect spot for
our tent," said Mickey.

"I don't think this spot is so great,"
Donald said. "There are probably wild animals
all around us."

Just then a skunk walked out of the
woods.

"Help!" Donald cried. "Get me out of here!"

"How can a little fellow like that scare you?" Mickey asked.

"Help me put up the tent before it gets dark," Mickey said.

Donald did as he was asked. But he did not like it. Soon night would come. Who knew what was hiding in the woods?

"*Whoooo!*" An owl flew out of the woods. Donald ran. Down came the tent.

"You're not much help," Mickey said with a laugh. "I will put up the tent. You stay out of the way, for now."

Donald sat on the end of a hollow log. Something moved inside it. The something ran out between his feet. "Save me!" Donald cried.

"Oh, Donald, a rabbit won't hurt you," said Mickey. "Come on. This campfire will cheer you up. How about some hot dogs and marshmallows?"

Suddenly they heard a noise.
"Wh—what's that?" asked Donald.
"It's only a raccoon," Mickey said. "He is
probably hungry. Here you go, little fellow."

"I won't sleep a wink all night," groaned
Donald. "There are wild animals everywhere!"
Mickey yawned. "Stay up if you want," he
said. "I'm going to bed. Good night, Donald."

Donald sat alone by the fire. He thought about what he might do if a great big wolf came out of the woods. He could chase it away with a stick. Or he could throw a frying pan at it. Or maybe he could grab it by the tail and throw it to the ground!

Donald waited and waited. But no wolf came. "This is the longest night that ever was," Donald said to himself. "Maybe a snack will help." He reached into a bag of apples. Just then there was a noise in the bushes.

Donald forgot about his snack. He climbed up a tree. He peeked down through the branches.

It was the raccoon again. He had come back for more to eat. And this time he had brought his whole family!

"Go away!" Donald shouted.

But before Donald could climb down the tree, the raccoons had hurried away with all of the apples.

Now Donald was really unhappy. And it was a long time till morning.

"I wish Mickey would wake up," he grumbled. "The time would go faster if I had someone to talk to."

Suddenly Donald had an idea. He picked
up a stick and ran around the camp. He hit
the bushes with the stick. He shouted loudly.
"Mickey, help! Wake up! It's a wolf!"
Mickey ran out of the tent. He was still
half asleep. "Where is it?" he asked.

"It was over there!" Donald pointed. "It was coming right at me!"

Mickey got his flashlight from the tent. "You hold the light," he ordered. "I will look for its tracks."

Mickey crawled into the bushes. After a few minutes, he got up. "There's nothing here," he said. "Are you <u>sure</u> you saw a wolf?"

"Well, it might have been over there," Donald said. Mickey took the flashlight and went to look around.

When Mickey came back he sounded
cross. "There is no sign of a wolf." He looked
at Donald doubtfully. "How big was it?"

"Bigger than the tent!" Donald said. "It was sneaking up on me when I saw it. I chased it—like this.

"You had better stay up with me, Mickey," Donald said. "Next time I might not be able to scare him off."

"Well—" said Mickey. Then he saw Donald's happy grin. "Did you make up this whole thing?" he asked.

"Who, me?" asked Donald. "There <u>was</u> a wolf," he cried.

Mickey did not know what to believe. "Don't wake me again unless you really need help," he ordered. "I mean it, Donald."

Donald sat down by the campfire. He peered out into the dark woods. Then he shivered.

Suddenly Donald jumped up.
"Mickey," he called softly. "Wake up,
Mickey. I think the wolf is coming back."
There was no answer.

Donald ran around the tent. *"Grrr,"* he growled. He tried his best to act like a wolf. Inside the tent, Mickey snored loudly.

Donald moved closer to the tent. *"Grrrr!"* he growled as loudly as he could. "Help, Mickey, help! The wolf is back!"

"I'm coming, Donald!" Mickey shouted. He
ran around the side of the tent. "It sounded
as if the wolf was right over here. Bring the
flashlight. I'll look for tracks!"

Mickey got down on the ground. He crawled back and forth. Then he stood up and glared at Donald. "I don't see any wolf tracks," he said. "But I do see your tracks, Donald. That was you growling like a wolf, wasn't it?"

"Listen, Mickey," Donald said. "I really wish you would—"

"No!" Mickey shouted. "I'm going back to bed. And don't you try to trick me again, Donald. I'm not going to get up—for any reason!" He went back into the tent.

Donald sat alone in front of the fire. He tried not to think about what might be hiding in the woods. "Maybe there really aren't any big wild animals out there," he told himself.

CRACK! A branch snapped in the woods.
The bushes shook. Two yellow eyes glared
out at Donald.

Donald jumped to his feet. "Who—who's there?" he asked.

A huge wolf ran into the clearing!

"*WAK!*" Donald leaped straight up in the air. He raced around the campfire. The wolf ran close behind him.

"M—M—Mickey!" Donald cried. "Mickey, it's a wolf! Help me!

"Oh, help!" cried Donald. He leaped
into a tree.
"Mickey, Mickey, help!" Donald shouted.
"It's a wolf! A real one! Honest!"

"No, it isn't!" Mickey shouted from inside the tent. "I told you not to try to trick me again." He put his hands over his ears so he could not hear the howls and growls. Then he went back to sleep.

For the rest of the night, Donald perched
high in the tree. At last the sun came up.
The wolf grew tired. It walked slowly away.

Finally Mickey awoke and came outside. Donald was just climbing down from the tree. "Mickey," he gasped. "There really was a wolf. Look!" He pointed to the tracks.

Mickey gulped. "I'm sorry you had such a bad time," he said. "But if you cry wolf when there isn't one, who is going to believe you when there really is a wolf?"

"Who—who—who?" echoed an owl.

This was too much for Donald. He ran for the tent.

A few minutes later, Mickey looked in. Donald was fast asleep.

"I bet that's the last time Donald cries wolf!" Mickey said to himself with a smile.